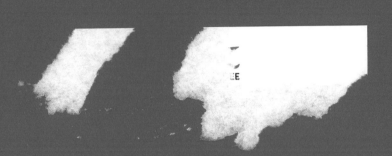

Lottie™

and the
Stolen Pirate Ship

Erika McGann

Illustrated by Leona Burns

THE O'BRIEN PRESS
DUBLIN

ERIKA McGANN has written numerous children's books, including the picture books *Where Are You, Puffling?* (illustrated by **GERRY DALY**) and *Standing on One Leg is Hard* (illustrated by **CLIVE McFARLAND**).

LEONA BURNS is a digital artist and graphic designer, born and raised in Raphoe, Co. Donegal. She studied in Atlantic Technological University (ATU) receiving a Bachelor of Arts (Honours) Communication and Graphic Design. Leona co-authored and illustrated *Moya's Night at the Zoo* for Dogs' Trust in 2022.

First published 2023 by The O'Brien Press Ltd,
12 Terenure Road East, Rathgar, Dublin 6, D06 HD27, Ireland
Tel: +353 1 4923333; Fax: +353 1 4922777
E-mail: books@obrien.ie
Website: obrien.ie
The O'Brien Press is a member of Publishing Ireland.
Copyright for text & illustration © Arklu t/a Lottie Dolls EU.
The moral rights of the author & illustrator have been asserted.
Copyright for layout, editing and design
© The O'Brien Press Ltd
Layout and design by Chris Rychter *www.chrisrychter.com*

ISBN: 978-1-78849-357-4

9 8 7 6 5 4 3 2 1
27 26 25 24 23

Published in

DUBLIN
UNESCO
City of Literature

Growing up with
O'BRIEN
obrien.ie

Printed and bound by Oriental Press, Dubai.
The paper used in this book is produced using pulp from managed forests.

Lottie lives on Branksea Island. It's the best place in the world.

It has a castle, and a lighthouse, and a forest, and a beach.

But best of all, it's got a pirate ship.

(Well, a broken old boat that got stuck in the sand.)

'Argh!' cries Lottie. 'I am the Pirate Queen.'

'And I'm the first mate,' says her best friend, Finn.

'I steer the ship, so I'm more important.'

'Grrr,' says Lottie.

Lottie's other best friend, Mia, is not on the ship.

She is making a mermaid's tail out of shiny blue shells.

'I spy a mermaid in the water!' Lottie yells. 'If we catch her, she'll give us some pearls to add to our treasure. Mermaids always have pearls.'

'Don't catch me yet,' Mia frowns. 'I'm not finished my tail.'

Lottie, Finn and Mia can't wait to play pirates and mermaids again. But when they get to the beach the next day, the broken boat has disappeared.

'My ship!' cries Lottie.

'*Our* ship,' says Finn.

'My tail!' sobs Mia.

The sand is all churned up, and the pirate ship is gone.

'Maybe the tide came in,' says Finn, 'and washed the boat away.'

'Uh-uh,' says Lottie. 'See those wavy lines in the sand? They're from the water coming in and out. And they don't come up this far.'

'Someone must have stolen the ship!' cries Mia.

Mia and Finn are very upset, but Lottie is determined.

'We're going to find our pirate ship,' she says.

'It must be somewhere on Branksea Island.'

Going on a hunt for a pirate ship is a big adventure, and Lottie decides they'll need a few things:

Binoculars
(for spying)

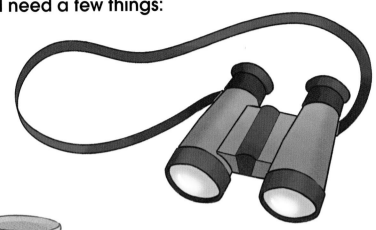

Comfy boots
(for walking and climbing)

A magnifying glass
(for spotting teeny, tiny clues)

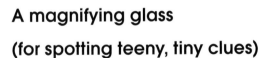

Snacks
(in case they get hungry)

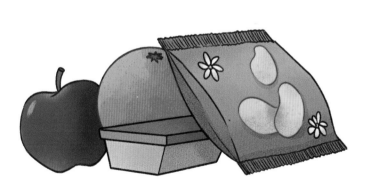

And Lottie's dog, Biscuit (because he loves an adventure).

Lottie and her friends start searching for clues. 'There are splinters of wood on the road here,' says Finn. 'They might be from our pirate ship.'

'This road leads to Branksea Castle,' Mia says.

'Maybe we should search there.'

'Good idea,' says Lottie.

'*Woof, woof*!' says Biscuit.

'Oh, Biscuit,' Lottie says, 'we *can't* play right now.

We've got a pirate ship to find.'

Branksea Castle is very old, and it's free to go inside and explore.

Lottie climbs the winding staircase to the top of the tallest tower.

Finn finds a secret door that leads to a secret room.

Mia crawls through a trapdoor to the dungeons underground.

But none of them spot their pirate ship.

'Ahoy!' cries Lottie, looking through her binoculars. 'I can see the fairy woods. That would be a *great* place to hide a pirate ship.'

'*Woof, woof*!' says Biscuit, but Lottie doesn't hear.

Lottie loves the fairy woods,

because she's very good at climbing trees.

Mia's *quite* good at climbing trees.

Finn doesn't like to climb trees.

Lottie's favourite tree has thick, curly branches.

It's the best tree in the forest.

'Bet you I can climb as high as the red fairy door,' Lottie says.

'No way!' says Mia.

'*Woof, woof*!' says Biscuit.

'What about our pirate ship?' Finn calls from the ground.

'Oh yeah,' replies Lottie. 'I nearly forgot! Let's search the park next.'

Lottie, Mia and Finn are playing on the merry-go-round

(because you can't go to the park and not go on the merry-go-round).

Mia is pushing it so fast she nearly falls over.

'Hmm,' says Lottie. 'I don't see our ship *anywhere*.'

'Me neither,' puffs Mia.

'I'm dizzy,' says Finn.

'*Woof, woof!*' says Biscuit.

Lottie sighs. 'Maybe we should search the village instead.'

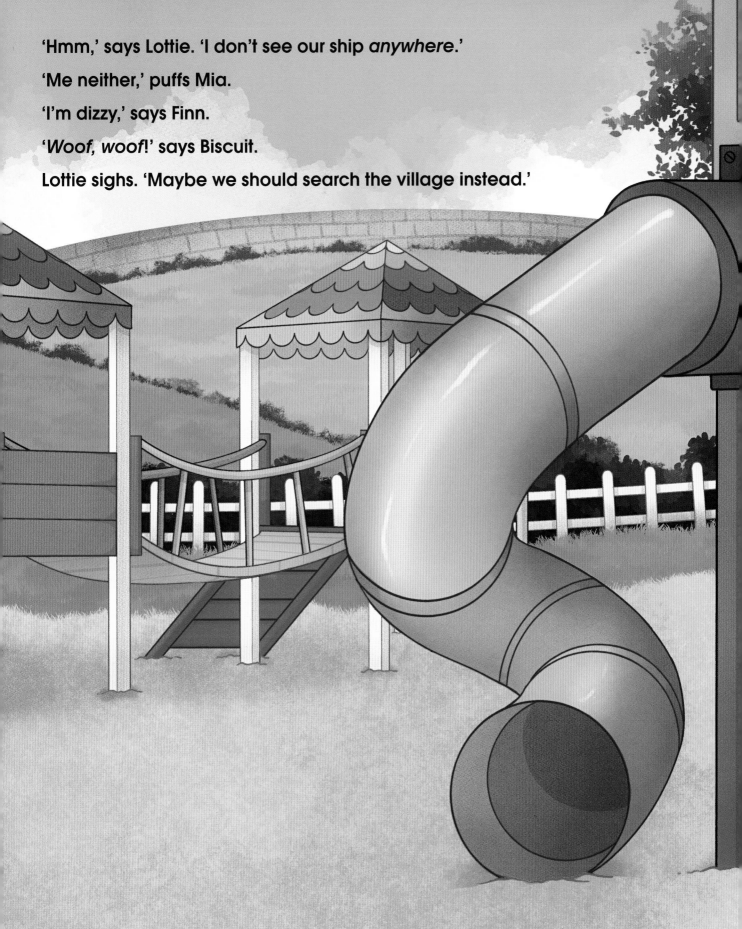

There's a lovely market in the village square.

One stall is selling hot chocolate. Another is selling popcorn.

There's even a stall that sells candy floss.

Lottie's mouth is watering.

'That candy floss smells *so* good,' she says.

'We've got snacks,' Mia reminds her. 'Right here in the bag.'

'They're not as yummy as popcorn,' says Lottie. 'And my tummy's so rumbly for popcorn.'

'We can't stop now,' says Finn. 'Come on. We have to find our ship.'

'*Woof, woof*!' says Biscuit.

'Alright,' says Lottie. 'But I don't see the ship around here. Let's try down by the pier.'

The pier is colourful and splashy and busy.

There are kites and boats and surfboards with sails.

'There are so many people,' Mia says. 'It's hard to see where *anything* is.'

HAVE A GO ON THE TUGBOAT!

Lottie nods. 'We'll never find our boat down here. We have to get up high.'

'But where?' asks Finn.

'The top of the lighthouse,' Lottie replies. 'You can see the whole island from there.'

'*Woof, woof*!' says Biscuit.

'Sorry, Biscuit,' Lottie says. 'Dogs aren't allowed inside the lighthouse.'

The lighthouse on Branksea Island is very, very tall.

'Oh,' groans Finn, 'I don't like being up this high.'

'But it's great up here,' Lottie says.

'We can see for miles around.'

'Maybe whoever stole our ship

has sailed it out to sea,' says Mia.

'Nuh-uh,' says Lottie. 'Our pirate ship was a broken boat. It couldn't sail on the sea for real.'

'Oh,' says Mia.

'Wait!' cries Lottie. 'I see it, I see it! Our pirate ship. It's on the street. It's painted blue. It's ... full of *flowers*.'

'And look!' says Finn. 'There's Biscuit, too. I think he must have found it first.'

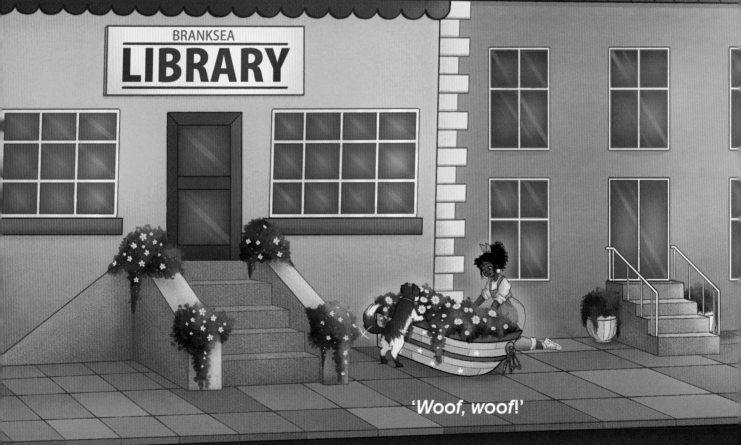

'*Woof, woof!*'

Annie is a local artist. She is standing beside the broken boat, and she looks very proud. 'Isn't this lovely?' Annie says. 'I found this piece of rubbish on the beach. I painted it and added stars, and made it look fantastic.'

'It wasn't rubbish,' Lottie says.

'It was our pirate ship. And we need it back.'

'I'm sorry, children,' Annie says.

'But I've worked too hard on this little boat.

I tried making it into a table, then a fairy house,

then a library, then a puppet theatre,

then a tugboat ride. And now it's *perfect*

as a flower bed.'

Mia and Finn want to argue with Annie,

but Lottie comes up with a plan instead.

Annie doesn't get how much *fun* we have on our pirate ship,
Lottie says the following day. 'We just have to help her understand.'
Lottie, Mia and Finn know that Annie loves art, so they use lots
of coloured chalk to draw piratey things around the flower-bed boat.
They cover the pavement in ships and parrots and pirate flags.

FOLLOW THE PIRATE TRAIL TO FIND THE BURIED TREASURE.

X

MARKS THE SPOT

Lottie, Mia and Finn draw a trail of pirate things on the path. It leads all the way to the beach. They draw a big red X on a rock, and then under the rock they hide:

A medal that Lottie won for swimming

Finn's old watch that still works

A gold gel pen from Mia's art set

And a letter to Annie, describing all the adventures they've had with the boat, and all the adventures they've still to have.

'When Annie sees this,' Lottie says,

'she's *bound* to give back our boat.'

The friends are excited. They wait and wait.

But home time comes, and there's no Annie.

'I guess she didn't like our pirate trail,' Lottie says sadly.

'Sorry, Lottie,' says Mia.

'Sorry, Lottie,' says Finn.

'*Woof, woof,*' says Biscuit.

But the next day...

'Our pirate ship!'

The boat is fixed and back on the beach.
It has a flag, and a parrot, and a skull and
crossbones.

'This is the best pirate ship *ever*,' cries Lottie. 'Thank you, Annie! Thank you so much.'

'Thank *you*,' Annie says, 'for your pirate trail and your buried treasure. I loved them! And you were right about the boat. It's much better as a pirate ship than as a flower bed. Have fun!'

Lottie, Finn and Mia have *lots* of fun. They play until the sun goes down.

'I am the Pirate Queen!' yells Lottie. 'And I spy a mermaid in the water.'

'I'll steer the ship that way,' says Finn.

'Wait til I've finished my tail!' cries Mia.

'*Woof, woof*!' says Biscuit.

And Pirate Queen Lottie smiles.

'*Aargh*!'